Flanimals

The Day of the Bletchling

by
Ricky Gervais

Illustrated by
Rob Steen

First published in 2007
by Faber and Faber Limited
3 Queen Square, London WC1N 3AU

Printed in England by Butler and Tanner, Frome

A CIP record for this book
is available from the British Library

ISBN 978–0–571–23851–4

2 4 6 8 10 9 7 5 3 1

Contents

This is absolutely everything
I know about Flanimals now.
In fact, a couple of bits
are guesswork.

Chapter 1

Blugs

As you know, the Flanimal kingdom is diverse and immense. Different species evolved and migrated in every direction. They flourished and dominated the plains, the forests and the mountains, the rivers, the swamps and entire oceans, from the shallows of Memptonia to the Hubba Numpy Depths.

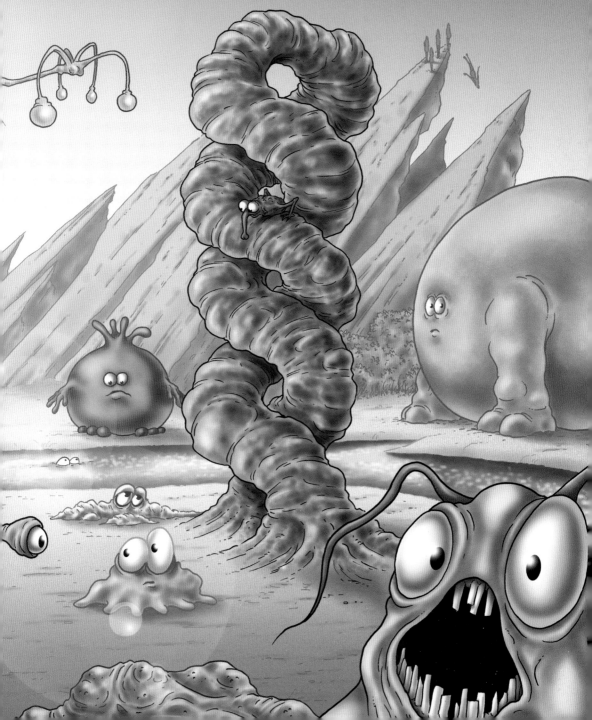

You've seen all that, but did you know Flanimals have also conquered the skies? No? Why? Didn't you look up? Well look up now, but watch where you're walking.

The first Flanimals to take to the air were the Blugs. Blugs are the most diverse class of Flanimal on the planet. They are also the most numerous, but there's still plenty of room because the sky is a big place. Probably the biggest place there is.

Zub

(Ticklus Hover Grebe)

Zubs, like Bants, are a specialised form of Vap.
They are fatter and more bumbloid, but this is no excuse.

Morphology

Blugs possess segmented bodies, with wings, legs, insides and outsides. They also have their ups and downs.

The Nervous System

They have a very nervous system. A central nerve cord runs from the legs and wings all the way through the body and up to the brain where it stops, has second thoughts, and runs all the way back.

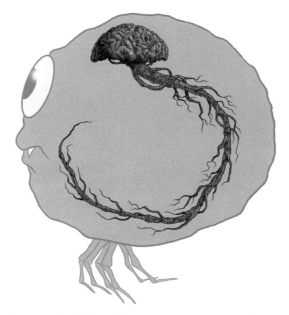

Figure A. The Blug nervous system

There are too many types of Blug to mention, but my favourites are Zubs, Bants, Frag Driers, Vaps, Movs, Hord Shufflers and Klunts.

Vap

(Swat Jasper)

Look, I could give you the whole spiel
on the Vap's evolution, anatomy, habitat,
behaviour, whatever, but let's be honest, you only need
to know one thing. The Vap is a nasty little swine.
Stay away from it.

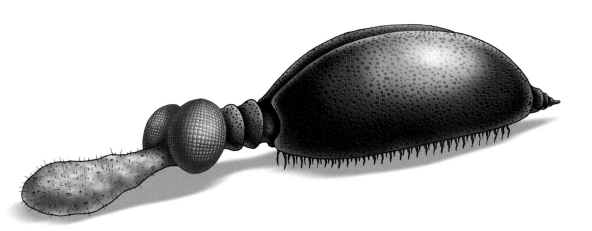

Hord Shuffler
(Probial Scram Addler)

The Hord Shuffler is a blind armadiddler.
Because of this it likes to scuttle around in dark places
where it has no disadvantage. They can usually be found
in bright open spaces. Well, they're blind . . . they've
got no idea where they are.

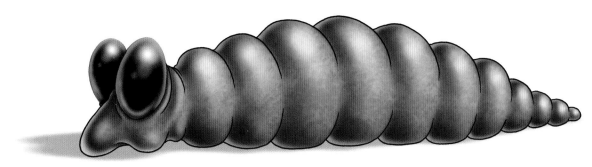

Monk Worm
(Vopine Stab Riddler)

The Monk Worm is the larval stage of the Frag Drier.
It looks defenceless and vulnerable doesn't it?
Even though it can see you coming, it can't move away
quick enough. However, it's got a trick up its sleeve.

If you cut a Monk Worm in half it grows back a new half. Unfortunately, it grows back two tail ends and the head end just watches the blind, double-bottomed spute sack wriggle around until it starves. Then the head dies as well. What a rubbish trick.

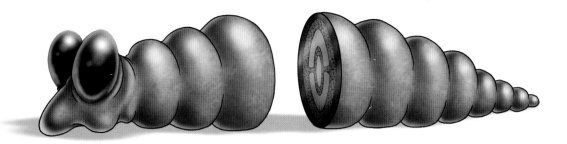

Figure A. Monk Worm cut in half

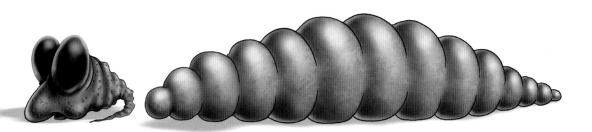

Figure B. Monk Worm regenerated

Frag Drier
(Vopine Stab Riddler)

The Frag Drier is a stealthy humbuzzler.
They fly around going berserk. They feel so free after
being a Monk Worm for so long, they go a bit over the top.
As a Monk Worm they could only go under the bottom.

Mov
(Mopey Flapjet)

This frappy flap oobrah is a frerbery bulb sniffler.
They don't look too bad until they land on you.
Then they just stick there. "Oh, a little Mov has settled on
my arm. I'll shake it off. Still there. Shake harder, still there.
Shake, shake . . . get off, arghhhh! It's still there. ARGHHHHH!
Help! Help! HELP! HELP! I'm scared to death!"
That's your lovely little Mov.

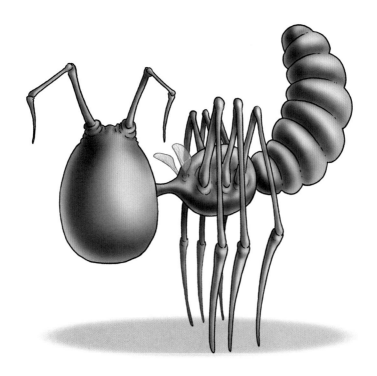

Bant

(Bantus Bantus Banti Banti Bant Bant)

Bants are small flying creatures that prefer
to walk and live underground rather than use their wings.
This seems stupid, but actually Bants are quite intelligent.
They are social Blugs, which is lucky as they live in nests
with populations of over one hundred thousand.

Bants get along for two reasons: one, they are all exactly the same, and two, they are always busy, so there is no time not to like each other. There is no such thing as a lazy Bant. If a Bant was spotted not doing much he would get a lot of dirty looks. This would shame him so much that he would bite his own head off.

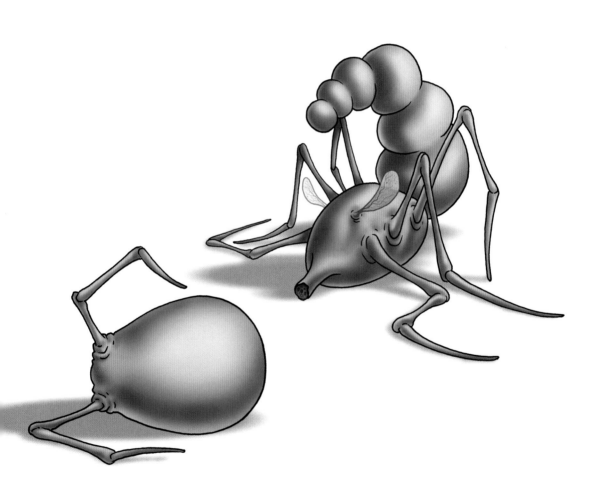

Every day Bants leave the nest looking for food. They spread out in all directions forming scout groups. When a group finds a good source of food it has to communicate the whereabouts to the rest of the colony. It does this by co-ordinated gesturing. They make signs and signals to indicate the direction of the food, like so.

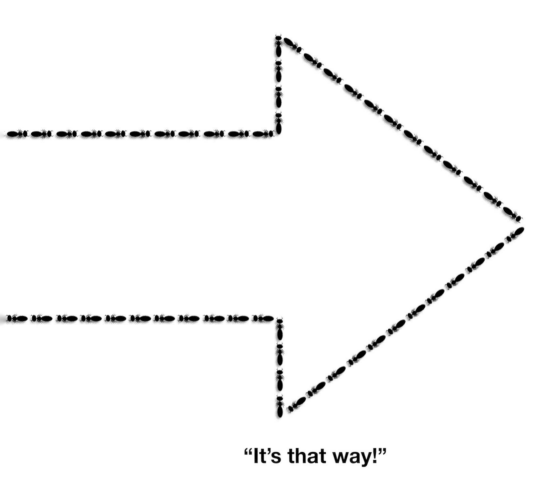

"It's that way!"

A Bant is suprisingly intelligent, for a thing without a face I mean. Some Blugs are less subtle in their behaviour.

From above the *Izunt* looks exactly like the *Iz*, or ground Klunt. This stops predators eating it. This is a bluff because it has no teeth, unlike the Flanimal it is trying to mimic. The real article has razor-sharp teeth, which it loves to sink into the neck of any Flanimal who gets close enough.

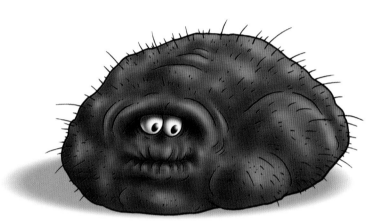

Pseudo Klunt
(Izunt)

Klunt
(Iz)

If the Flanimal the Klunt is trying to bite doesn't get close enough it's still not a problem. The *Iz* will just walk over to the Flanimal and sink its teeth into its neck anyway. As you can see, it really is a proper Klunt.

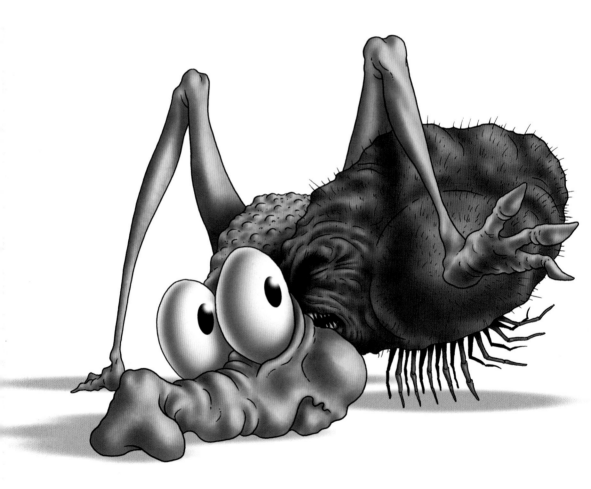

A Klunt biting a Spleg's neck

Flanimals coexist brilliantly. They breed and eat each other. It's a good system. Well, it's not a *good* system. Being eaten isn't a good thing, but it works. Not for the thing being eaten of course, but that's life. And death. So, all the Flanimals live and flourish together on this jam-packed planet, on the land, in the air and in the depths of the sea.

Goof Mump about to be eaten by a Roxstrambler

Some are weird. OK, let's be honest, they're all weird. If a Flanimal wasn't weird that would be really weird. Some are ugly. Let's face it, most of them are ugly. Even to each other. And some are terrifying. But there is one Blug that is weirder, uglier and more terrifying than any other Flanimal that exists or ever has existed.

The Bletchling.

Chapter 2

The Super Blug

If you were to feed the brain of a Bletchling to another Flanimal it would go mental, killing everything in its path. Even if you mashed the brain up and liquidised it and injected it into a Glonk, the Glonk would smash your face in. This is because the Bletchling's brain is evil on a molecular level.

Of course, if you were to feed the brain of the Bletchling to another Flanimal it would mean that YOU were already mental.

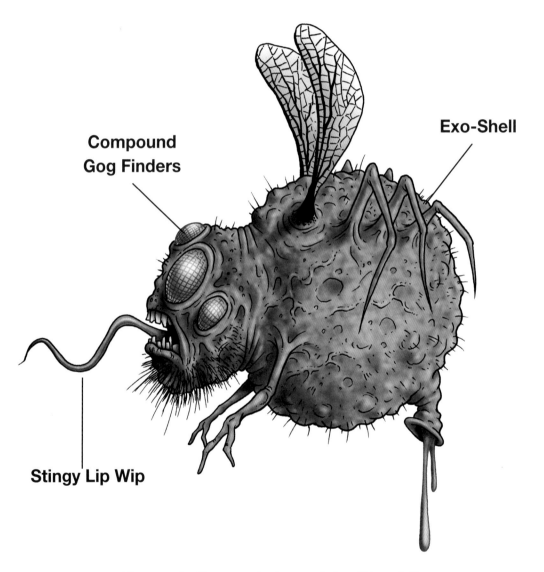

Compound Gog Finders

Exo-Shell

Stingy Lip Wip

Figure A. External view of the Bletchling

Why would a sane person ever do something like that? Having a brain that isn't in a head at all is mental. Serving it as a meal is even more mental. Eating a Bletchling brain sends things mental. Trust me. You don't need to test this. OK? Good.

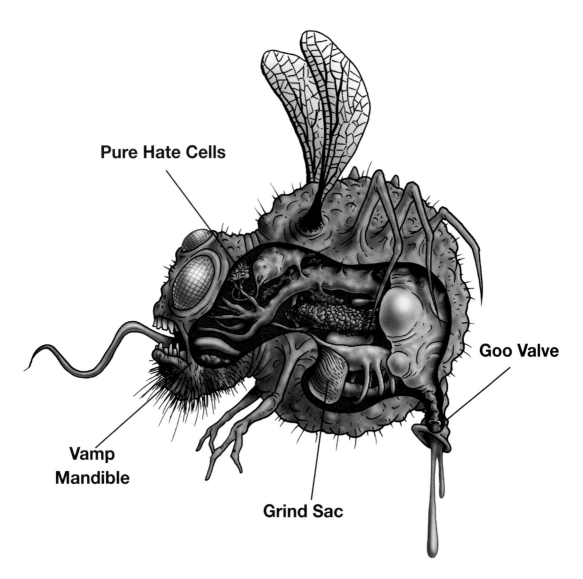

Figure B. Internal organs of the Bletchling

The sheer sight of the Bletchling would paralyse you with fear. The sound of its buzz would make you ill. Its blood would burn your skin. Even the sound of the Bletchling's name is annoying. If you say it fifty times in the dark it can send someone crazy. Try it. Wait until your dad is asleep and creep into his room screaming "Bletchling" a few times. I bet you he won't be happy.

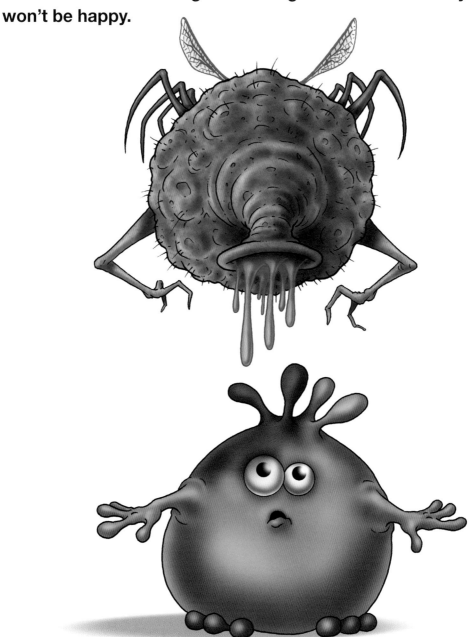

Chapter 3

The Day of the Bletchling

One day something strange happened. Well, every day something strange happened, but this day something particularly strange happened. The ground wriggled and writhed, a vomboid stench punged the air. One whiff of the giant inpsychosect made Flanimals spew and moan across the land. The Bletchlings were on their way.

Slowly they emerged like invertebrate zombies. No bones means more room for evil in their murderous living carcasses. First hundreds, then thousands, then millions, then hundreds again. They waited as blood pumped into their wings.

Ready now, they buzzed and buzzed a
terrifying hum of death. Then away, up into the sky.
Well, actually just a few feet off the ground, but high
enough. High enough to swarm over every living
creature on the planet and destroy.
Destroy everything!

Slowly, painfully, without feeling, without thought and without asking. Although asking would be the wrong way to do it. Most Flanimals would say no, which would be disappointing to the Bletchling. Also, it would take too long. No, this is the way to do it if you want to wipe out every single species on the planet. Flying, not asking, and all together is the way to go. Teamwork.

So they swept across the land, blanket terror, merchants of death spewing their wares onto the hapless prey. The Hapless Prey is a type of Sprot, by the way.

Hapless Prey
(Munjy Snack Fodder)

A jiverly unger ployb. With nowhere to hide
it draws attention to itself by sweating like a Klunt.
Incidentally, a Klunt sweats because its blood is
always boiling with anger.

Anyway, they vomit their caustic goo onto all Flanimal life. First it feels sticky. Very sticky. So sticky you're stuck. Then it burns, and finally it turns you into Flanimal stew. The Bletchling then simply descends and sucks up the liquidised victim.

No Flanimal was safe. No Flanimal had any defence. They needed a miracle to survive. They needed a higher power to save them. They all prayed to Grob but nothing happened. Nothing happened because there is no Grob. They all felt so stupid believing in something so ridiculous and far-fetched. Something that defies logic and is so impossible but gives hope to a futile existence.

Well now existence is all they have got, so they had better start thinking for themselves. Magic can't help them; hope can't save them. They need a hero, something real. Something real brave. Chaos reigned. Blungings blunged in all directions, Splunges splunged and Clunges . . . I wanted to say Clunges clunged, but clunged is not a word.

Out of the bleak stepped a loan figger. A Bleak, by the way, is a hugebolfrugerous gobbler. It can swallow anything. Unfortunately it has no digestive fluids so Flanimals thrive in there. They love it!

Bleak
(Nash Natterphibia)

One of the more populous creatures to live inside the Bleak is the Loan Figger. A Loan Figger is a flap happy ambloid, but now the chunkling has to stop. Time to get down to business.

"Let's fight back," he barked loudly.

"Could we?" they all thought.

The Loan Figger stepped into the baking sun and picked up a rock.

Loan Figger
(Web Chump Solaris)

A Bletchling approached. All the Flanimals held their breath . . . Well it stank out there.

Wait . . . Wait . . . Now! With all his might he hurled the rock at the Bletchling. It was a pathetic throw – short arms. The rock barely reached the Bletchling. It bounced back and smashed the Loan Figger in the face, which was quickly followed by the Bletchling squirting him with goo.

Dead.

That was very disappointing.

One Flanimal can't make a difference. They have to fight together. What if they all make a stand? And that is what they did. Armies of Puddloflaj, no longer cowardly wobblers, they wobbled bravely into war.

Grundits, like tanks, linked arms
and staggered towards battle. Glonks
. . . well, Glonks did absolutely
nothing, but they did it together.
It was magnificent!

It was to be the most
bloody war the planet had
ever seen – carnage –
but still they fought.
They fought like warrior Flans.
Baby Mernimblers were launched
like metamorphic missiles.
They changed into adults in
mid-flight, to rip and tear
at the Bletchlings.

Then it got nasty. But they fought on.
Tired, injured, dying. It was working.
Gradually the Bletchlings dwindled in number.
The Flanimals were winning.
Hooray! Hooray . . .

Oh no, hold on. That was just
the tip of the iceberg. There were
millions more emerging and
taking flight.

Chaos. Flanimals ran in all directions. No one Flanimal ran in all directions, but between them every direction was covered. Even up and down. Well, they didn't run up and down, they jumped up and down, which is pretty pointless.

Also, it's easy to jump up, but much harder to jump
down, especially if you're already on the ground.
Jumping down if you're already on the ground means
you end up sort of crumpling yourself to death.
You can bury yourself. Some did this, some buried
each other. Some jumped in the rivers to escape the
Bletchling but they were just eaten by Strankulators.
Oh, I forgot to tell you about the Strankulator.
It doesn't matter now. Nothing matters now.

The Day of the Bletchling happens every thousand years. Millions of Bletchlings emerge and reign terror for just a few days, but this time was different. Extraordinarily large amounts of the eggs survived due to the mild winters on the planet, and this time there were billions. Don't get me wrong, I love a mild winter, but not if it's followed by this sort of apocalyptic summer.

Would anything survive?

Chapter 4

No!

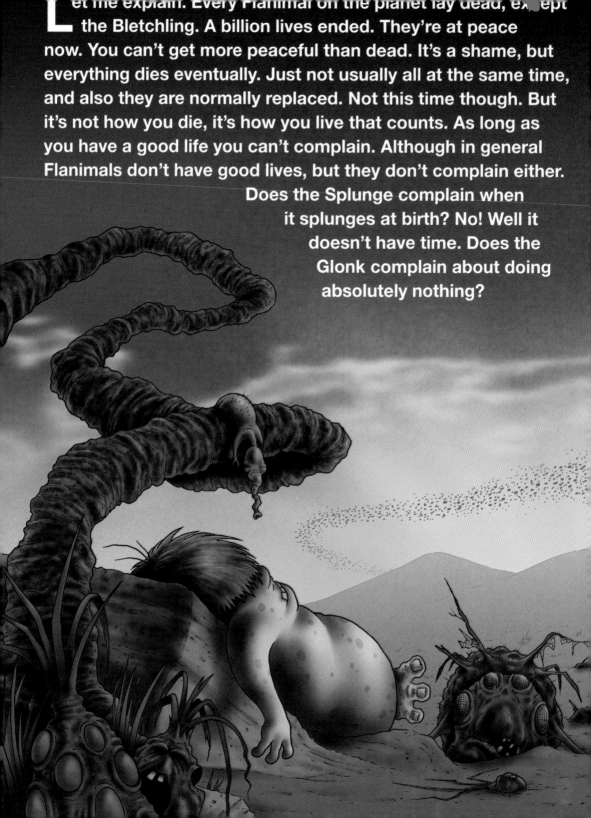

Let me explain. Every Flanimal on the planet lay dead, except the Bletchling. A billion lives ended. They're at peace now. You can't get more peaceful than dead. It's a shame, but everything dies eventually. Just not usually all at the same time, and also they are normally replaced. Not this time though. But it's not how you die, it's how you live that counts. As long as you have a good life you can't complain. Although in general Flanimals don't have good lives, but they don't complain either. Does the Splunge complain when it splunges at birth? No! Well it doesn't have time. Does the Glonk complain about doing absolutely nothing?

No. If it complained it would be doing something, wouldn't it?
The Plamglotis may be complaining, you just can't make out
what it's saying. The Bletchlings had destroyed everything,
but they had also destroyed themselves. When they next
emerge there will be nothing to sustain them. They will be
wiped out as a species. So now it would be a dead planet.
No Mernimblers, no Honks honking, no Splunges and no
Glonks . . . well, they didn't do anything anyway. I still liked
them though. I liked every Flanimal actually.

Millions and millions of years of evolution turned to dust. What a waste of time, although, can you waste time? Time goes on forever, so even if you waste a bit there's loads more to come. Too much. More than there's been already, and there's been a lot. So all I'm saying is there's a lot of time, but it's how you spend it. It's not a waste of time if you pack lots of stuff into it. Good stuff though. Don't pack bad stuff into time, that's a waste of time.

I hate bad stuff happening, even though it's natural. I wish things were always nice. They're not! Live with it! Just don't add to it. Flanimals do stuff because they've evolved to do that exact stuff. It's not nice to see an adult Mernimbler rip a Flemping Bunt-himmler to pieces, but it's not nice to see an adult Mernimbler starve to death either.

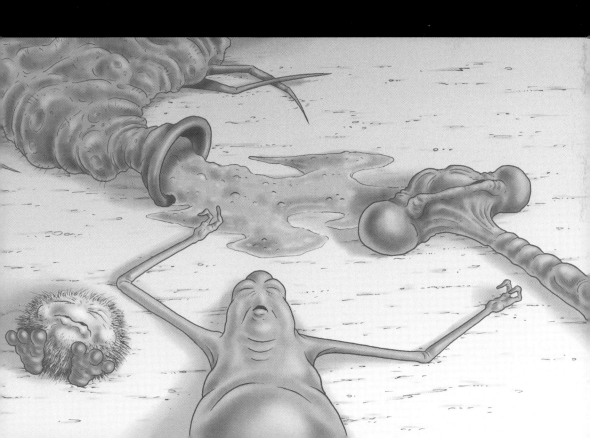

Flanimals were great. Even the ones that annoyed me.
They couldn't help it. It wasn't their fault, it was their nature.
You are what you are. What are you? I told you what you are.
You are what you are, and they were what they were.
They were magnificently evolved creatures, all different
and living together on a lonely planet.

Now nothing.

Oh, wait a minute. There's some Splorn. It was too small to be noticed. But Splorn's not very interesting, is it? That was the very first attempt at Flanimal life. Everything was better than Splorn eventually. No, this planet is rubbish now.

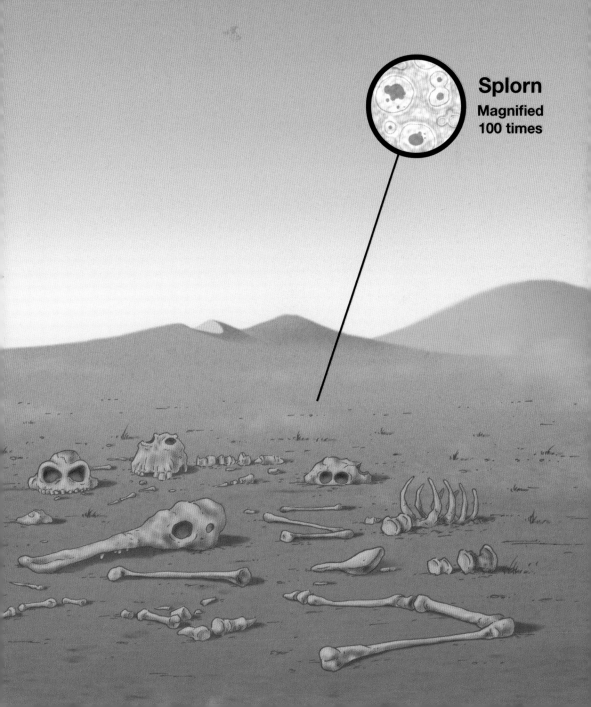

Splorn
Magnified
100 times

But hold on, if Splorn evolved once, maybe it will do it again. Maybe it will take longer this time. Will some be completely different, or exactly the same? It will take a very long time but there's no reason why this planet can't thrive again. Millions and millions of different creatures. Strange, colourful, dull, stupid, pointless, wonderful, wonderful creatures.

Flanimals.

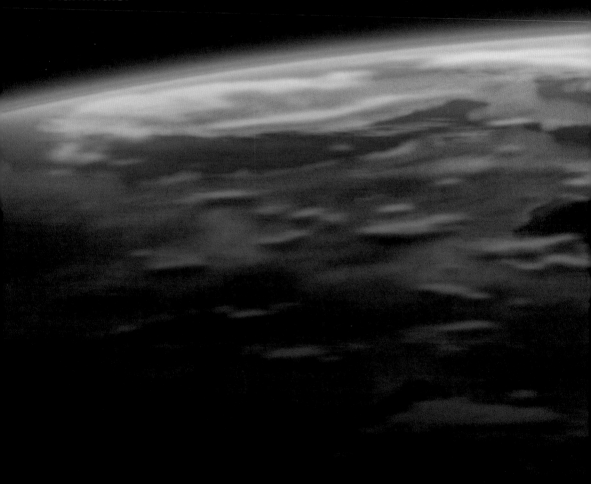

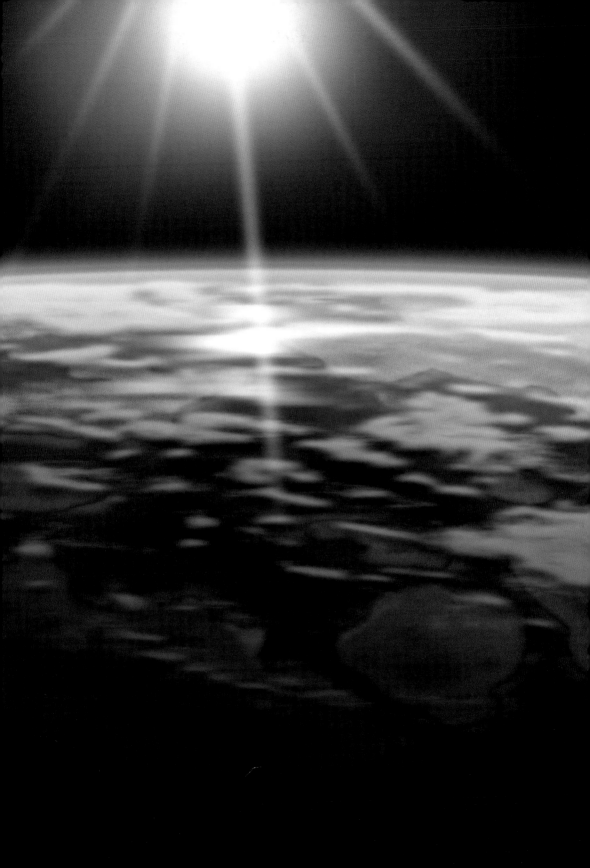

Flanimal Scale Chart

Human   Bant   Bletchling   Frag Drier   Goof Mump

Hapless Prey   Hord Shuffler   Klunt

Loan Figger   Monk Worm   Mov

Pseudo Klunt   **Strankulator**   **Vap**   **Zub**

Bleak

We'll come back in a
while to see how life is getting on.
I'd give it a few million years to
see any visible developments.
But who knows, there might be some
really interesting stuff happening
by next Christmas.